Loving a Stranger
Playboy MF Romance Short Story
Author: Hannah Sterling

From the Author:
Thank you for purchasing this book.

Table of Contents

Loving a Stranger
Description

Lisa Cooper needs some fun and excitement before she takes her bar exam. That summer is her one chance at a wildlife, and when she meets the billionaire playboy Nate Jenson, she knows he's perfect for her.

Their one-week whirlwind romance is what she needs. It's exciting, it's wild and hot, but what happens when she starts to crave more?

Nate enjoys women, but it never gets serious.

Lisa Cooper changes something in him from the minute they meet. Maybe it's those eyes, or the way she speaks, he can't tell. But he's never met a woman so beautiful with a heart so pure.

There's passion and romance, but what does it take to turn a one night of passion to a long-lasting romance?

Chapter 1

Lisa spent the past three hours at the airport clearing her luggage. She finally made it to Hawaii after all the hassles. A delayed flight, terrible turbulence, and a non-working luggage roller at the airport. Clearing had been difficult and finding a cab to her hotel her been worse.

Finally she was here, and it was fun time, which was all that mattered.

She turned to her friend, Maggie, sitting to her right at the bar. Maggie was engrossed in singing along to the Doja Cat lyrics playing in the background, and her glass of cocktail was half empty.

"Loosen up, Lisa," Maggie said to her, then started rolling her hands in the air. "It's a fun two weeks, the last one you'll probably have in your life once your career starts. Make mistakes now and regret them later." Maggie was speaking on top of her voice, and Lisa was laughing because she thought her friend looked and sounded ridiculous.

Hawaii is all about fun, she had told herself on the way here. After years in law school, and acing her bar exams, she deserved some fun and she was going to get it in two weeks before she resumed at her dream job as an intern in New York's most prestigious law firm... Holland's Law Firm.

Tonight, she was going to live wild. Maggie had no idea what she had planned for her night.

As Lisa looked around the bar, she scouted for hot males. If she could land one stranger, then she could fulfill a life-long craving to have one passionate night of fun.

People do it all the time, it's not a big deal. Besides, she was single, beautiful and she needed to get laid.

Maggie picked another glass of cocktail, while Lisa downed her shot of brandy and sighed.

Her eyes wandered around some more, then landed on a man sitting at the far-left corner of the bar. He wore a leather jacket, his thick mass of dark hair blended into the darkness of the club's dimly lit setting, and she couldn't see much of his features because it was the side of his face she could view from where she sat.

Maggie rose to her feet and pulled the man sitting with her to the dance floor. Lisa watched them dance for a bit before she turned to look at her handsome stranger again. The man was still sitting there, and now he was speaking to a woman who couldn't keep her hands off him.

Lisa cringed as she watched him try to take the lady's hand off his chest, but the lady returned it, and gave him a cocky smile. she shook her head and looked away. She wasn't so good at flirting either, but at least she understood when a guy a wasn't into her or what she was doing.

She finished her brandy, got up and walked towards the man, telling herself she was probably saving him from a night long boredom with the blonde he seemed disinterested in.

When Lisa got to where he sat, she draped one hand over his shoulder, and spoke. "Hey baby..."

The man turned to look at her immediately. Her eyes merged with his intense dark ones, and she felt a shiver rush through her. The zap left a tingle that reached the pit of her stomach. Her skin flushed instantly, and her breath hitched in her throat.

"I missed you, sugar. What took so long?" he said, and swooped his hand around her waist, pulled her closer to him and whispered. "I've wanted to do this all night."

He brought his lips close to hers, and her pulse skyrocketed even though he kissed just the corner of her mouth then pulled back.

The blonde woman huffed, rolled her eyes then walked away. Lisa stood there, rooted to one spot, and reeling from the effect the man had on her. His hand was still wrapped around her waist, his eyes moved from hers to her lips and then back to hers again, then he smiled.

"I just saved you from a night of boredom, you owe me a drink now," she said when she could find her voice.

"I love it when a woman asks," he replied with a smirk, then motioned for the waiter. "Brandy? Bourbon?" he asked.

"Scotch," she replied, wanting to taste something different.

Their drinks arrived after a minute. Lisa downed hers in one go, and when she heard him chuckle, she turned to him. She could make out his physical features now. He had a pointed nose, and full lips that made her crave his kisses.

Lisa blinked, not wanting to come off as too forward, but it was obvious that she was gawking at him now. He smiled again and she saw the deep dimple in his left cheek. His eyes squinted at the corners, he tilted his head to one side, and spoke. "Wanna play make believe?" he asked.

"What?" Lisa replied then laughed. "Isn't that a game for kids?"

"It is," he replied. "But you see I have this meeting in a few minutes here, and it sems like the client would take me more seriously if he knew I had a serious girlfriend."

"You want me to play your girlfriend?"

“For one hour,” he answered. “Make believe,” he added, then smiled again. “You already started it, so we might as well continue.”

Lisa accessed him closely, then she shook her head and nibbled on her lower lip. “You’d have to buy me another drink for that,” she said.

“I’d buy you as many as you want,” he agreed, then motioned for the waiter the second time. “Just tell me what you need.”

His hands brushed hers as they both reached for their glass at the same time. Another jolt of electricity moved through Lisa, and the slow hum rising in her blood told her she had found the perfect man for her extraordinary night of fun.

Chapter 2

One hour later, the woman sitting with Nate Jenson was tipsy. He loved the way she smiled as she spoke even though her words were starting to sound like a slur. Her eyes kept wandering to his, and she kept touching his arm flirtatiously. Each feel of her slender fingers on his arm made his body jump with excitement.

Mr. Herard and his wife had stopped by the bar to pick up some documents I brought with him from the office, but they hadn't stayed for long like Nate anticipated, and he had more time with the woman now.

He was enjoying the sound of her voice too, and he didn't think he had heard anyone sound so husky before.

She was talking about her time in Hawaii. "It's my first time here," she said as she lifted the glass to her lips again. the smile on her lips were seductive, Nate couldn't stop staring at her even though he had just met her, and he could tell that she felt the same rich tingles he did because when their hands had touched earlier she had gasped, ten sighed and her cheeks had a gained a lovely shade of crimson.

He admired her. The lovely curve of her lips painted a bold shade of red, her blonde hair, and blue eyes and the creamy smoothness of her skin. She wore a red dress, the same shade as the color on her lips, it was a sleeveless one and he could see her creamy cleavage.

Nate enjoyed woman. He liked looking at them, he never made them think he wanted anything other than their body, and that had worked for him for a long time now. He considered himself a painfully honest man. There was no need to make any woman think he could give them anything more than a good time. It was a standard for him.

"So you've never been on a trip before?" he asked when she took a pause from her long talk.

"Never..."

"What else haven't you done?"

"I've never been skinny dipping," she said, then laughed when he arched a brow.

"You're kidding."

"Never kissed a stranger," she continued listing.

"Now that one has to be a joke."

She laughed hard and shook her head. Nate felt the slow build of desire in his loins as he watched her and listened to the breezy sound of her laughter.

"Never had sex with one either."

"No one-night stands?"

"I plan to have one tonight." Her words were bold enough to make his body respond in a hard way. She was direct... he liked that. She was seductive in an innocent kind of way and compared to the blonde throwing herself at him moments before, he found this woman more intriguing.

Maybe it was because he sensed there was a part to her that she considered plain and boring. Even though he couldn't imagine her being any of those things.

With those eyes, and the cures of her body exposed from the little tight red dress she wore, he knew she could excite almost any man.

When she moved closer to him, he didn't stop her, and when she put a hand on his arm, his gaze dropped so he could stare at her lovely sender fingers. Nate's body hardened a bit, and he smiled again.

"I plan to also," he told her, then met her eyes again before he lifted his right hand to her face, caressed her cheek, then let his thumb press down on her lower lip.

She moaned, and it was the sexiest sound Nate had heard in a long time. He spent most of his time at work, defending his clients in court rooms, and winning cooperate lawsuits. He always took whatever chance he got to relax, and here one was presenting itself to him as usual.

"Maybe we should skip the rest of the night?" he suggested. "My suite's nearby."

She smiled, he knew she was tipsy, but still conscious, so he leaned closer to her, and nibbled on her ear lobe before whispering. "I could teach a few things tonight if you'd let me."

Her hand moved to his chest, and he pulled back to stare into her eyes, but his gaze touched her lips instead. He saw them move softly as she spoke. "Teach me."

Nate didn't need any more approval. He rose to his feet, took out a wad of cash and placed it under his glass for the waiter to see, then he took her hand and led her towards the exit.

When they got to his Chevrolet, he held the door open for her, then got in his side and drove them to his hotel suite. The second they got inside, she tossed her clutch to the ground, moved to him, and draped her hands around his neck.

Nate didn't hesitate to kiss her. She tasted like mint, her lips were moist and soft, and they made his nerves come alive. He couldn't think of a better way to spend his evening.

Her skin smelled like lavender as he peeled off her clothes, and she moaned when he feasted on the pulse beneath her neck. She raised her head, stared into his eyes then looked past him to a corner of the room.

“Oh my God,” she suddenly exclaimed, then pulled away from him and hurried to where he kept his awards arranged on a shelf. “Is this...”

“Alexander Award,” he told her.

She gasped, dropped that one then moved to the other. “And this...”

“Robert P. Wilkins, yes.”

“Oh shit... are you?” she stared at the award then back at him, her eyes wide, and cheeks beet red. “You’re a lawyer... you’re *that* lawyer? The only one who’s won a Robert P. Wilkins in 15 years?”

Nate smiled, then moved close to her so he could take the award from her delicate hands. He put it back on the stand, then slid his hands into the pockets of his pants. “Yes, that’s me... Nate Jenson.”

Her eyes widened further, and she turned away from him.

“I’m fainting right now!” she exclaimed as she bounded on the bed.

Nate laughed at the shocked look on her face. “I get that a lot,” he said to her. “That shocked reaction when people find out I’m a lawyer and also a scholar.”

“You’re too good looking to be that smart,” she said. “It’s almost surreal.”

It was Nate’s turn to laugh, and he sat on the bed next to her, then spread his hands out on the matrass.

“How did you do it?” she asked, then folded her legs up in front of her and rested her chin on her laps. “I mean... I’m fresh out of law school and I barely have a social life. How did you manage it all?”

Nate sighed, then weighed his answer for a second before he said to her. “I didn’t do much… I just did whatever I wanted when I wanted to.”

Chapter 3

They spent the rest of the night talking, and even though Lisa still felt the burning intensity of her arousal, being with him like this was so much more fun.

Lisa was sitting close to Nate now and staring into his eyes as he told her of his experience in law school.

"I put in my best in everything because I wanted the best out of everything. When I was young my mother... she had to leave my dad at some point because they couldn't agree on anything, so growing up with just her made me realize life wasn't a bed of roses early enough."

"What motivated you? I mean it sounds like your motivation came from more than just a competitive streak."

He passed when she asked the question and rubbed the back of his neck before he spoke again. "It did. I just needed to make more for myself... a name and all for myself. I needed to be remembered, I felt the urge to become this great person that no one could look down on. I guess it's because of how I watched my mom struggle while growing."

"You did make a name," she said. "Everyone knowns Nate Jenson, whcn I passed my bar exams I told myself I was going to work under the best law firm and make a name for myself to."

"Did you get in?" he asked, wanting to know more about her. Nate had completely lost track of time and it didn't matter that the events of the night had taken another course the second she had seen his award. He enjoyed listening to her, hearing her talk, and pour out all her ideas.

He watched her hand movements as she spoke earlier and couldn't tear his eyes off her face. She was the most beautiful woman he had ever seen, and he didn't even know her name yet.

"I got into Holland's law firm," she said, and lay down on the bed. Nate didn't think twice before he joined her to lie down. He folded his hand under his head and gave her his full attention.

They spent the entire night talking, and Nate fell asleep by her side at some point without realizing it. when he opened his eyes in the middle of the night, he saw her sleeping soundly by his side, curled into a ball with her lips slightly parted.

His heart did a slow dive in his chest and warmth filled him as he stared at her. He couldn't explain it, but it was the first time he had a women in his bed and he hadn't touched her yet.

He took a long minute to stare at her and admire her fully. She was still wearing her underwear, and her hair was plastered all around his pillow. Nate touched some strands, and let it slide through his fingers.

Her hair was silkier than he imagined and when he leaned closer to her, he caught the blend of lavender and roses on her skin.

He wanted her, but it was unlike the feelings of desire he usually had when he was with an attractive woman. Nate watched her for a long time, then he pulled the sheets over her body to cover her skin.

She sighed and murmured some words in her sleep. When she shifted on the bed, he moved closer to her, and put his hand under her head so she could rest on his arm.

Nate stroked her cheeks, admired her some more, then dropped his head to the bed and closed his eyes.

The next morning he was alone in bed when he woke up, and the smell of strong coffee hit his nostrils. He sighed in and rolled over to his side on the bed. For a second he couldn't understand why the scent of coffee woke him up, but when he opened his eyes and saw the clothes scattered on the floor, he instantly remembered her.

Nate jerked off the bed then and hurried out of his room to the kitchen. She had her back to the doorway, and she was swaying her hips from side to side as she stood in front of the kitchen table.

"What are you doing?" he asked after staring at her for a while. She turned around then, holding a mug in one hand and a spoon in the other, then she grinned, and it seemed like his world stopped because he had never seen anyone more charming.

"Morning," she greeted in a cheery tone. "I'm making coffee. How do you like yours?"

Nate stared at her, she was wearing his black shirt, and it stopped just above her back side, exposing her thighs and the rest of her long, slender legs.

She was still grinning at him while he stood there blinking, in shock of what was happening. She looked so much at ease, and after the length conversation they had the last night, he understood why she would feel that way.

It was his first time to speaking about himself so much, it felt like he had written an autobiography.

"How do you like your coffee?" she asked again.

"Black," he answered.

"Awesome... I love mine black to."

When she turned around again, Nate hesitated for a bit before he walked into the kitchen fully and sat at the table. It was his first time having a woman over who stayed till the next morning, and then made him breakfast. But then again, this wasn't just any woman. She was also the first one he didn't get to business with after bringing her to his suite for the night.

There's something different about her, he thought as she brought his coffee to him, set it on the table and smiled at him again.

Nate knew he had to figure out what it was about her that made him so interested in her person more than her body.

Chapter 4

Lisa finished her breakfast but did not move from where she sat at the table with Nate. He took her hand after some time and led her to the living room.

She was wearing his shirt, but his touch on her hand made it feel like she was naked. Heat rushed through every part of her, brought her nerves alive and made her dance with the stirring arousal deep inside her loins.

"This was my very first award. I was in high school, and I scored a goal that brought my school's team to the national finals," Nate said.

He then took her through the array of awards and prizes arranged in his living room. She admired them after each other and imagined what it was like for him when he was younger.

"Did you ever do anything fun besides work and school?"

"I play the cello," he told her.

Lisa asked, turned to him, and arched a brow. "The cello?" she asked rhetorically. He gave her a ridiculous smirk that made her laugh hard then, and Lisa flung her head back for a bit till the spasms of laughter rocking through her subsided. "The cello? Not a violin?"

"Yes, you won't believe I can play till you hear me," he said to defend himself, and she giggled for a bit, then tried to picture an image of him with the instrument.

He left her in the living room, then returned with his cello.

Lisa sat when he did the same and she listened to him play for the next ten minutes. At some point she started humming to the song he was playing and moving her head from one side to the other. She was enjoying the song so much that she got lost in his eyes when he stared right at her.

She admired the way his fingers moved with the cord as he played. His voice was a soft melody, and it warmed her heart, made her crave to listen to him that way for a long time.

When he finished, Lisa clapped her hands and rose to her feet.

"I've never learned to play an instrument," she told him when she sat next to him. "I think you just inspired me."

"What inspires you usually?" he asked. "What inspired you to become a lawyer?"

She shrugged. "My dad," she answered in a solemn tone, remembering the events that led to her father's death three years ago while she was still in law school. "My dad was one before he passed away and my mom... I guess she always believed I could do whatever I set my mind to do, so she was more of a supporter than anything else. He passed away three years ago, and I hate that he won't get to see me start my internship at a law firm."

"I'm sure he's still proud of you regardless," Nate said to her, and his words served as comfort.

Another hour passed, and he told her off his passion for justice. It was surprising to learn that someone with his looks and personality cared so much about the law. Lisa knew there was a lot to learn from him.

By afternoon they were still in his living room, and Nate noticed first, so he suggested. "Care to do something fun?"

Lisa immediately agreed. Her two weeks in Hawaii was for fun right?

They went to the beach side and spent the day watching a group of dancers perform the hula. She had always loved the traditional dance, and watching it live was more exciting than she had ever imagined.

Lisa rose to her feet and joined in the dance at some point. She moved her waist to the beat and spent her time making sure her hand movements matched that of her waist.

Nate cheered for her at some point, then he, motioned for him to join him, but he refused, shaking his head before he asked her to come back and sit beside him.

Their time at the beach was the best fun Lisa had enjoyed in a long time.

Talking to Nate was easy, they connected on a deeper level, and it was her first-time enjoying time with a man this much. It was like they had known each other for longer than a day now, and she wasn't interested in doing anything other than spend time with him.

She tried out a few local dishes sold at the stands, the luau stew and strawberry mochi while Nate had a Saimin.

By the time they returned to his hotel site, she was exhausted, but the day didn't end there.

She sat in bed with Nate, neither of them feeling the rush to sleep or do anything else but sit there and listen to each other talk. Lisa fund that she was lost in his conversations.

That night they played a game of chess in his living room. Nate was on a winning streak, and she was sulking because he was better with his calculative moves.

They finished a bottle of red wine, and she went to the bar to get another one. As she walked back into the living room, she caught Nate's eyes on her. his gaze moved from her legs to her face, and it settled on her lips for a while before he met her eyes again.

She could still feel the buzzing intensity of their attraction. From the second they met at that bar it had been there, but why had neither of them made the first move.

Lisa remembered his kiss, and how intense it had been. She knew if he touched her again she would give into him, but they were enjoying each other's company much more than anything else, and she was starting to think that when they finally kissed again, it wouldn't stop at just kissing, and their passion would be the most explosive one she had ever felt.

Chapter 5

Nate placed a call to his friend the next morning. Lisa was in the bathroom washing her hair and singing to herself. He was listening to her sot sounds while he stood near the window and spoke to his friend and at some points when she stopped singing to hum, he smiled to himself because he knew she was dancing.

"I'll be back by next weekend," he said to Tim. "Have everything in place for the press conference and make sure our clients are in the loop. We need to salvage the situation before it gets any worse."

When he ended the work call, he walked to the bathroom, leaned against the door frame, and watched Lisa. She wasn't aware he was standing there yet, and it was fun to watch her.

Their instant click still amazed him. since he brought her to his suite three days ago, every second had been exiting and fun. Nate couldn't remember a time when he had enjoyed someone's company this much, and it wasn't even like they had known each other a long time.

Lisa must have sensed his presence because she stopped singing and turned to look at him. Nate smiled at her, then entered the bathroom fully. He walked over to where she stood and handed a towel since she had completely washed her hair.

She put her hand over his as he started drying her hair, and he stopped when he was certain most of the water was squeezed out. Nate lowered his hand and started into her eyes for a second. The smile on her face started to dwindle a bit, and he was lost in her eyes before he looked at her full lips.

"Breakfast?" she asked, still looking at him. the first thought that crossed his mind was one insanely seductive. He would love to make love to her for breakfast and get lost in her eyes and arms till the end of the day, but for reasons he couldn't understand he held back again.

"Let's go somewhere."

He led her out of the bathroom before she could protest, and once in the room she pulled her hand from his.

"All I have here is my red dress. I haven't been out of your suite since I came in that night, and..."

"That's not a problem, all I have to do is place a call."

She was still staring at him when he took out his phone and placed a call to a friend. Jennifer Tuchez was a woman he had dated for a while when he lived and worked on a case in Hawaii. Since they separated a year back, they had kept in touch because he always remained cordial with everyone.

Nate's social network was a chain. His honesty made it possible for him to keep relationships with women and end them without hassles. The one rule he had for such occasions was simple: Never promise what you can't fulfil.

Nate's detachment from long-standing relationship was the core of his network. His vast number of female friends always came in handy at times like this.

Jennifer arrived at his suite one hour later with several clothes for Lisa. She was a fashion icon here on the island and a few times in the past, he had needed her help like this to.

When Lisa came out of the room dressed in comfortable jeans and t-shirt, she smiled and swirled around on her feet to show off the outfit.

“You look amazing,” Jennifer squealed, and Nate nodded. He smiled at Lisa again and gave her a thumbs up.

They spent their morning out strolling the local market. Lisa had a fascinating way of expressing her amusement. Whenever she saw something she liked, there was a spark that came to her eyes, and her tone became lighter almost sounding like a baby’s voice.

She also laughed a lot. Her free-spirit and light-heartedness were the things he admired most about her. Also each time he stared at her, there was a rush of adrenaline that coursed through him and reminded him of how beautiful she was.

They tried out the local cuisine at the market to. Nate especially loved the spicy Pipi Kuala, and Lisa’s intolerance for spicy food was a cause for concern so he made her stick to the corn dogs and mac salad.

After eating, they joined a group of tourist watching the street dancers at a corner. Lisa mimicked some of the dance moves, and even though she didn’t get them right, he still found her adorable.

They went on a boat ride and ended up at the beach that evening to admire the sunset while strolling the sandy shores. Nate was holding her hand in his, and at some point he linked their fingers, wanting to feel a stronger connection to her.

Lisa looked at their joined hands while he did, and he grinned at her before tightening his grip.

They sat by the shore after that, she stretched out her legs in front of her, and he moved closer so he could feel the heat of her body next to his.

"These past three days are the best I've ever had. It's been so much fun, and I don't think I've had this much fun before."

"It's the same for me," he said, facing her as he smiled.

Nate couldn't control the way his heart stuttered in his chest when she smiled back at him. He loved the curve of her lips, and how her blue eyes clung to his. His chest swelled with warmth and flutters that made him feel like a high school kid having a crush.

He had felt attracted to women before, but not once had he craved being around them for this long.

In that moment, Nate realized one thing. He was falling for Lisa Cooper, and it wouldn't be long before he was completely head over heels.

It's bound to happen eventually.

Chapter 6

When they returned to his suite, there was no need for words. The slow passion brewing between them since that first night came to light again. This time when Nate kissed her, there was no holding back.

Lisa didn't want to stop. She slid her hands into his hair and moaned when his steady hands moved down her back and pressed her into him. His body was harder than anything she had ever felt, and he was touching every angle of her back, pulling her closer and at the same time making her feel things she had never felt.

His tongue drove into her mouth when she parted her lips for him. at the same time she felt his hand on her backside. He spread his palms over her and pressed harder, so she felt the swell of his erection on her lower abdomen.

Lisa moaned again, and it was his turn to groan when she let her tongue start a slow dance of pleasure with his.

Nate scooped her off her feet and her legs wrapped around his waist. He rocked his hips into hers, made her cry out, then moved so her back was against the wall.

Nothing felt better than having his erection press the spot between her legs where she was growing wet for him. even though her jeans were in the way, she could still feel the rise of her arousal, and she wanted him to touch her there.

Lisa drew her lips from his and arched her neck so he could kiss the sides and feast on the pulse beneath her ear lobes. Hs hands on her bottom kept cupping her, and when she moved a little, his responding growl made her shiver.

"I want to do things to your body," he whispered hoarsely into her left ear. "Make you feel things you'll never forget."

His words made her tremble and burn hotter for him. He was stroking the flames of an unquenchable fire inside her, and it would take more than just those words to make her feel sated.

When he moved her to the bed, she brought him down with her and plastered her lips to his again. her hands moved under his shirt, and at the same time he slid his hands to her back, unclasped her bra skillfully, and pushed her blouse off her head.

Her bra came off and his lips covered one nipple in the next heartbeat. Lisa cried out when he nibbled on the tip, the licked the spot and sucked the bud. Her legs started to quiver on the bed when his fingers found its way into her jeans.

Nate pushed the jeans down her waist and took off her underwear with it. she was naked under him now, and she wanted to level thigs up a bit.

Lisa worked on the buttons of his shirt with haste. Once his bare skin was exposed, she started kissing him all over. His fingers massaged her clit, she moaned and spread her legs wider giving him access to her body.

She sucked in a deep breath when the tip of his middle finger pushed into her already wet entrance. Instinctively, she bucked her hips, and he slid all the way in.

Nate groaned because she touched his erection. The tip was wet, and that meant he was just as aroused as she was. she couldn't wait to make his body feel the same tension hers felt. Every stroke of his finger, and kiss from his lips made her quivering mess. She was hot and bothered for him.

When he slid his finger out, she gasped, and touched his full length. She ran her hands down it, loved the way he trembled with his groan and flung his head back.

Lisa flipped over so she lay on his back and straddled his thigs. She lowered herself onto his tip slowly, and his hands clamped over her waist to guide her.

She was moaning when he impaled her with his full length, and her toes curled into the sheets. Her body accepted him wholly, and the feeling of liquid ecstasy that coursed through her was amazing.

Lisa started a slow ride with her hips. He groaned in response to every dance of her body over his, and she moaned when he held her steady so he could thrust in and out of her with precision.

He turned again, made her lie on her back, and he lifted her hips with both hands, so she was at his mercy. Every thrust of his hips took her closer to the edge. She kissed him deeply, her hands moved into his hair, and her body was his.

When he pounded his hips into hers one last time, she cried out and climaxed around him. Nate's groans were deep. He buried his face in the croon of her neck and rocked into her hard.

She sighed and kissed the corner of his lips, then he kissed her forehead, gathered her close and rolled over to his side on the bed. It took a long time for their breathing to return to normal, and he his hands didn't stop caressing her.

Lisa fell asleep in his arms, and it was the most peaceful feeling in the world. She woke up to him kissing her, and touching her body, arousing her all over again, and she was instantly lost in the heat he created.

They made love till the early hours of the morning, neither of them able to get enough of their passion. Nate fell asleep by her side after and Lisa lay there, looking at him, and admiring every of his features.

Her heart swelled in her chest when she remembered all they had shared in the past three days, and she couldn't control the flush that flowed through her entire body. She knew she was falling for him now, and that was a problem because eventually this peaceful haven they had created for themselves would come to an end and they would each need to go back to their individual lives.

What would happen then? What happens to our bond and passion?

Lisa didn't think she wanted to find out. it's best I end this before either of us gets hurt. That way she could leave with her heart intact before it was too late to stop herself from loving him.

Chapter 7

Nate woke up alone in bed the next morning. He sat up when he touched the other side of the bed and found it empty, then he looked around in search of Lisa.

Usually in the mornings, she made breakfast, and she loved having coffee in the morning, so he should have smelled its strong scent by now, but the air was fresh and there was no hum in the bathroom to indicate she was taking a shower.

He looked to the nightstand where she kept her phone and found it empty. Instantly his heart did a slow dive that left him breathlessly in pain for a second.

Nate walked out of his room to check for her around the suite. Lisa was nowhere inside. He considered waiting, perhaps she went out to get somethings, but that wasn't necessary because everything she could possibly need was in here in his suite.

How could she do this? How could she leave after the passion we shared last night? Is this all she wanted? Was it just a one-night thing for her? A short-lived passionate experience?

His mind was reeling with different thoughts and in all the scenarios he hated that she had left him without a word. It was his first time feeling this innate sadness of realizing you were used, and Nate didn't think he could get used to it.

The first time he had cared about more with a woman, she didn't feel the same way.

Standing alone in his living room then, he combed his fingers through his hair, sighed and closed his eyes. He couldn't work through the pain clouding every other feeing in his body.

How could she just leave like that?

He stood there for a long time, and a voice in his head told him to wait for a bit. He was clinging to the hope and possibility of her leaving because she needed to get somethings or meet with someone. Nate was hoping she hadn't just left him in the middle of the night.

By afternoon when there was still no sign of her, it was obvious that she had.

Nate didn't know how to deal with the ache that coursed through his heart. He had been enjoying their time so much he had completely forgotten it was not his real life. Lisa was just an amazing woman he had met in a bar and spent the best four days of his life with.

Why did she need to stay? She had a right to leave. what they shared was a whirlwind affair. A romance that could never surmount to anything. Besides knowing she was a law intern and a brilliant woman; he didn't know anything else about her.

They had shared so much with each other in four days, but it didn't mean she was still not a stranger. Nate filled his mind with thoughts that could help him safely process the hurt and loss he was feeling. They weren't important emotions because Lisa was not a woman he knew deeply.

I can get over her.

Considering she had left without even saying goodbye, he knew she was thinking the same thing.

Nate concluded then that he could get her out of his mind. He called his friend and assistant and left instructions for his next flight back to New York. He was cutting his vacation short because he suddenly felt the urge to work, or maybe it was because he couldn't imagine himself having any more fun here on the island.

I guess this is how it ends.

Even though he trying to come to terms with the fact that Lisa had left without a word, he still couldn't fight the feeling of loss. He hated that je was feeling it, but he couldn't control his heart.

Nate returned to New York two days later. The second he arrived at his law firm, he got to work. There wasn't a long list of client's cases waiting on his desk. He was senior managing partner of the firm, so he mainly handled high profile cases. Nate usually had free time on his hands to go golfing with clients and attend charity events with other business he was tryin to sign a deal with, but this time, he had to focus on something to take his mind off Lisa.

He found a case to fix his entire focus and attention into, and he spent the next week working. Nate figured he wouldn't have the time to think about Lisa if he was working, but that didn't work out as he had planned.

He thought about her every second of the day, and at night when his subconscious was at its weakest, he dreamt of her.

The next Friday evening, he was working late at his office, and his assistant brought in take outs for dinner before she returned to her desk to sort out the files he had given her.

Nate took a break to relax, and when he closed his eyes, thoughts of Lisa entered his mind again. He sighed, rubbed the back of his neck, and since he was unable to get her out of his head, he decided to feed his curiosity.

Without re-considering his options, he went on social media and searched out her name: Lisa Cooper.

Nate scrolled through many pictures before he finally stumbled on her.

Her smile was the same, and seeing it made his heart clench tighter in his chest. He realized how much he missed her when he started watching the videos on her page. Hearing her laughter again made him relax a bit, and it was then he realized he needed to be close to her again.

Nate didn't know what to do yet, but he was certain of one thing. He was in love with this woman, and he couldn't get her out of his head.

Even though she had run from him, he knew he wouldn't rest till he could be with her again. Nate wanted her, and he was going to find her so he could make sure she knew that.

Chapter 8

Lisa hated that she couldn't focus on the task at hand. She drove to the court room, and arrived there earlier than she scheduled time for the hearing with her senior, but turned out she had to wait for a current session toe end before she went in.

She waited in the hallway, and watched lawyers go about their activities. Her role as a junior associate at Holland's Law Firm was a chance for her to advance her career in many ways and she was taking every chance she could get.

Maggie was also at the court room that day, and Lisa was hoping to see her before she went into the room herself. Their opponent was a senior partner from a competing law firm in New York. It was Lisa's first time in court, and she was hoping for it all went smoothly even though she was going to be more of an observer on the case.

They didn't even let me see the case files.

Thirty minutes later, it was time for their case, so she entered the court room with Stanley Krater her direct superior. When she took her seat beside him, and waited for him to do the same, she glanced to her side and her eyes landed on the opposing counsel seated in the other end of the court room.

Her heart lurched when she saw him. Color drained from her face, and she had to look away before he noticed her. Lisa's palms turned sweaty, and she blew out air from her lips to steady herself.

It's Nate, she thought. Her mind was already spinning in different directions, and she was literally praying he didn't notice her either, but what were the chances? When she was on the opposing side?

The judge came into the room and the hearing began. Lisa remained glued to her seat while her senior started with his opening statement, then called out a witness for examination before presenting his evidence.

When it was Nate's turn, he rose to his feet, did the same as her senior then stepped forward to hand over his evidence so she could cross-examine the witness of the stand.

His eyes landed on hers then, and Lisa froze in her seat. she couldn't think of anything else but him, and the intensity of his yes that clung to hers for a millisecond before he looked away and continued with his statement.

When she left his suite weeks ago she had been so sure she would never see him again regardless of how much she cherished the memories of their time together, and how much she missed him.

Her whirlwind romance with Nate was bound to end either way, and she had done the right thing by leaving that morning before he woke up, but what was this pounding in her heart as she thought about it now?

The court hearing ended for the day with an adjournment, and Lisa hurriedly left the court room even before Stanley did. She made it outside to her car and was about getting in when Nate caught up with her.

He pushed her door close when she opened it, and she was forced to turn around and look at him.

"Lisa," he said, his voice the same husky sound she remembered.

Heat flushed her skin, her eyes widened, and her cheeks heated up. She knew the beet red color there would be visible, especially when his eyes drift over her face to her lips and then back to her eyes again.

He was looking at her the way he did every time they were together in the past, and her pulse was hammering now, making her temples ache and her had swoon.

"You left," he said to her as she stared at him in shock. Lisa could smell the strong scent of his cologne, and it made her shiver because she remembered how much passion he had invoked in her from the start.

"I had to," she replied to him, then sucked in a deep beath to steady her lungs. "It was bound to end anyway, I'm sure you know that."

Nate shook his head. His eyes left hers for a second, and he sighed before he looked back at her. "Not for me," he replied. "I didn't want it to end, and I didn't know you were thinking of ending it."

"Nate ..."

"This isn't just coincidence, Lisa," he continued, interrupting her before she could say anything. "This is more like fate. The fact that we met here again like this, it's fate... You know it is."

Lisa swallowed after she licked her lower lip nervously. "Fate?" she repeated, and he nodded.

"I've never been in love before," Nate said to her. "But I'm falling for you Lisa and I have been from the start."

Her heart leapt with joy as she stared at him, her eyes searching his, and she was trying to control her erratic breathing because she needed to make sense of his words.

"I've never been in love either," she told him, then lowered her lashes a bit so she could stare at his lips. "We barely know each other... This is crazy."

"I know it is," he agreed. "I was going to find you, I didn't know what to do after you left so I pretended and tried to forget, but I couldn't get over you and I was going to hire a PI to find you. Thank God I found you sooner..."

Lisa's face was merely inches away from his, and because she had missed him so much too she silenced him by pressing her lips against his for a soft kiss.

Nate stopped talking then, and the corner of his lips lifted before he took the lead and kissed her back. She didn't care for where they were, and anything else that could happen. What she was sure of was that she wanted Nate just as much as he wanted her, and that had to count for something.

Chapter 9

The second she walked into the court room, Nate had seen her, and he was not denying that his heart had ached at first before he realized it was his chance to tell her what he was feeling.

It couldn't be just coincidence that they ran into each other again like this.

It's fate... we are meant to be.

He pulled back from her, his entire body still craved more of her kiss and her taste, and he needed her to understand that this was more than just a fling for him even though he just told her what he was feeling.

"I have to get back to work," Lisa said then laughed a little before she licked her lower lip and looked into his eyes again. "Nate..."

Her breath fell from her lips with a shudder, and Nate quickly stole another kiss before she could say anything else.

He looked around him, then stepped back to put some room between them.

"Tonight, let's have our first date," he suggested. "I don't want to waste any more time, I just want to be with you. We're meant to be, Lisa... I know we are, and I have never been so sure about anything else in my entire life."

She nodded in agreement, then he reached into the pocket of his suit and took out his phone.

Nate got her number before she got in her car and drove off. He was still standing there minutes after, wondering how he got so lucky to have found her like this again. His entire body was quivering from their kiss, and his heart wouldn't stop thumping so fast.

His response to her had been this way from the start when she had walked up to him in that bar, wrapped her hands around his neck and pretended to be his girlfriend just to save him from the blonde woman he had no interest in speaking to.

Looking back at that night now, Nate couldn't suppress the smile that came to his lips. Lisa had been bold and adorable back then, and she still was.

He took a moment to breathe deeply and control himself before he walked to his car, got in and drove away.

The rest of the day, Nate couldn't control the excitement cursing through him. He thought of Lisa the entire time, and anticipated night when they would meet for their date.

After a meeting with his board directors, he got off work, stopped at his penthouse to freshen up, then he called Lisa.

Nate picked her up from her apartment, then they dined at a five-star restaurant for the rest of the night. The entire time he listened to her talk, he couldn't get his eyes off her, and that feeling had him certain that he could spend his entire time watching her like this.

Nate hadn't ever imagined himself in love, but he loved the tingles in his heart and the way his entire body flushed just from being this close to her. The sensations were intense, and he didn't mind one bit.

I'd do anything to see her smile like that always.

"I love it here," she said when she finished admiring the place again. she was holding her wine glass in one hand, and grinning at him. Nate let his eyes drift down her body, and he admired the sleeveless black dress she wore.

"I love you," he replied, not taking his eyes off hers for even a second. Her lips parted when she gasped, and he smiled because he loved how she looked at him with those intense dark eyes. "I mean it."

She extended her hand, placed it over his on the table and caressed the front of his palm. The moment tensed up then, and Nate knew he wanted her while he sat there.

"We should go to my penthouse," he said to her, still holding her hand and admiring her face. They left the restaurant together and headed to his house. Once inside, Nate took her in his arms, and kissed her deeply.

He backed her towards his room, not wanting to waste any second without having her in his arms. She returned his kisses passionately, and his body responded to her.

"I didn't stop wanting you," he confessed when he pulled off her dress and admired the curve of her body in her underwear. "Not once did I stop craving your touch and your scent. Even when I was heartbroken that you left without saying goodbye."

"I didn't want to," she replied. "But I was falling for you, Nate and I didn't know what to do. It was supposed to be one night of fun, but we ended up... I ended up falling in love with you before I even realized what was happening."

He kissed her again, took his time to explore her lips before he stepped back so he could look at her again. Nate ran his hands down her body then she slowly undressed him before they made it to the bed.

They were lost in each other's embrace the second their bodies touched the bed. The heat of the moment was more than anything he had ever felt. It was intense and made him shudder with pleasure and pent-up energy.

Nate kissed her deeply as he thrust into her the first time. She gasped and arched her body to meet his, then wrapped her legs around his waist and held him close.

She matched his passion and exceeded it. Being with her was mind-blowing and when it was all over, he made love to her all over from the start.

The next morning, Nate woke up to the strong scent of coffee just like he remembered, and he went into the kitchen to meet her. She handed him a mug and he smiled as he took it from her, sipped the dropped the mug on the table so he could pull her into his arms again.

They shared another long, passionate kiss, and he lifted her off the ground, placed her on the table, and moved in-between her thighs. His hands slid under the shirt she wore so he could touch her bare skin, and he slowly unbuttoned it before he pulled her closer to him again and hooked her legs around his waist.

"I can never get enough of you," he told her before nibbling on her lower lip and kissing the side of neck.

He carried her out of the kitchen and into his bedroom again. Lisa was giggling when he put her on the bed, climbed in after her and rolled over so she was on top of him.

"I love you, Nate," she whispered as she put her hands on his cheeks. "It's still surreal to me but I'm getting the hang of it."

"I love you to," he said to her. "I know this is just the start of our adventure together... I'm sure of it."

Lisa leaned down and kissed him this time, then she led slowly started grinding her hips over his and his body grew harder in response to her touch.

He laughed as he pulled her down on him and pinned her to the bed.

This was the start of their passion and he looked forward to what the years ahead held.

Epilogue

One year later:

Lisa had always loved weddings, but she found that she loved island weddings more, and hers was a dream come true.

Nate was smiling as he stood in front with his best man, and as she walked the distance between them, her heart pounding, she couldn't control the smile on her face. It was like her life was starting, and she knew the years to come with Nate were going to be as magical as the last year they had spent together.

As she stared at Nate standing there, she remembered the night they met here in Hawaii, and the craziness of the few days that followed. Lisa could never have imagined that she would fall in love with her perfect stranger, and now that she knew all there was to know about him, she didn't regret her decision one bit.

I fall deeper in love with him every day that passes.

When she reached his side, he extended a hand to her, and linked their fingers. She loved having him this close, their hands linked together tight with neither of them wanting to let go.

Her best friend, Maggie, was right standing with her, and Lisa smiled at her when she glanced over her shoulder and saw Maggie grinning wide.

"You ready?" he asked, his eyes not leaving hers for a second. "This is the start of the rest of our lives."

Lisa dragged in a deep breath, then nodded, and grinned at him. "I know, and I am as ready as I'll ever be," she replied before facing the priest in front of them.

They proceeded to the vow sharing, and she vowed to spend the rest of her life with him, loving him, and cherishing him.

"I vow to love you till the rest of our days and be with you no matter what."

Nate did the same, his eyes remained on hers, and the warmth she saw there made her inside tingle and bubble with excitement of what was to come. She loved him... very much, and nothing could change that.

After the ceremony, Nate drove them to their new house, and Lisa was giggling hard as they made it inside kissing like their lives depended on it. He ran his hands down the side of her body and kissed her deeply again before she could escape him.

When he lifted her off the ground and carried her into their room, Lisa wrapped her arms around him and gave in to the passion already brewing between them. His breath was hot on her face, and his hands skimming down her body filled her with heat till she was shivering and burning for more of his touch and kisses.

"I love you, Nate," she said, not wanting to hold back any part of herself from him now.

Her love was true, and strong, and she was certain it would last... Always and Forever.

THE END

www.ingramcontent.com/pod-product-compliance
Lightning Source LLC
LaVergne TN
LVHW040929150826
845672LV00007B/2277

* 9 7 9 8 3 5 3 2 9 3 7 9 8 *